Around the World Tales

Edited by Carol Huey-Gatewood, M.A.Ed.

Publishing Credits

Rachelle Cracchiolo, M.S.Ed., *Publisher*
Conni Medina, M.A.Ed., *Editor in Chief*
Nika Fabienke, Ed.D., *Content Director*
Véronique Bos, *Creative Director*
Shaun N. Bernadou, *Art Director*
Carol Huey-Gatewood, M.A.Ed., *Editor*
Valerie Morales, *Associate Editor*
Kevin Pham, *Graphic Designer*

Image Credits

Illustrated by: front cover, pp.1–7 Anais Goldemberg; pp.8–11 Alexandra Huard; pp.12–15 Mariana Ruiz Johnson; pp.16–19 Shahab Shamshirsaz; pp.20–23 Rogerio Coelho; pp.24–27 Tony Ganem; pp.28–31 Elena Iarussi. Courtesy Luma Creative Limited. All rights reserved.

Library of Congress Cataloging-in-Publication Data

Names: Huey-Gatewood, Carol, editor.
Title: Around the world tales / Carol Huey-Gatewood, editor.
Description: Huntington Beach, CA : Teacher Created Materials, [2020] |
   Audience: Ages 12 | Audience: Grades 4-6.
Identifiers: LCCN 2019026459 (print) | LCCN 2019026460 (ebook) | ISBN
   9781644913208 (paperback) | ISBN 9781644913208 (ebook)
Subjects: LCSH: Children's stories. | CYAC: Short stories.
Classification: LCC PZ5 .A6427 2019 (print) | LCC PZ5 (ebook) | DDC
   [E]--dc23
LC record available at https://lccn.loc.gov/2019026459
LC ebook record available at https://lccn.loc.gov/2019026460

5301 Oceanus Drive
Huntington Beach, CA 92649-1030
www.tcmpub.com

ISBN 978-1-6449-1320-8

Table of Contents

The Polar Bear Son · 4

Maui Goes Fishing · 8

Why Whales Swim in the Sea · · · · · · · · · · · · · 12

Smell of Soup, Sound of Money · · · · · · · · · · · 16

The Mouse Merchant · · · · · · · · · · · · · · · · · · 20

The Shark God · 24

How the Milky Way Came to Be · · · · · · · · · · · 28

Book Club Questions · · · · · · · · · · · · · · · · · · 32

The Polar Bear Son

In an Inuit village on the edge of the Arctic Circle, there lived an old woman. She had no family, so the people of the village looked after her. They caught fish for her and shared their meals with her. Despite their kindness, the old woman was lonely and wished for a family of her own.

One day, the old woman was walking along the icy seashore, when she saw a tiny polar bear cub. When no mother came to claim it, the old woman scooped him up in her arms. "Poor little thing," she said. "You will be my son," she whispered, smiling at the little bear. She called him Nanuk.

She took the bear cub back to her igloo. Over the coming weeks, a strong bond grew between the old woman and her polar bear son. The children of the village all loved Nanuk, too. Every day, they came to visit the old woman, and they played with Nanuk in the snow. Her igloo echoed with their laughter.

As Nanuk and the children grew older, they taught him how to fish and hunt for seals. Nanuk turned into the smartest and strongest hunter. Every day, he would go out to hunt, and then he would return home with armfuls of salmon for the old woman.

She was happy to repay the kindness of her neighbors and would hand them fresh fish, saying, "My Nanuk is the best fisherman in the village!"

But the men of the village soon grew jealous of Nanuk. "He's making us look bad," they grumbled. "There is no room for another hunter in this village." And so, the men decided to get rid of Nanuk.

When the children heard what their fathers were planning, they ran to the old woman and told her.

The old woman set off to visit every igloo in the village, where she begged the men to leave her son alone. "If you harm him, you will break my heart," she cried. But the men were too proud and stubborn.

With a heavy heart, the old woman returned home. "You must leave here, Nanuk. The men don't want you here, and your life is in danger. You must go and never return."

The old woman and Nanuk hugged each other tightly. With tears in his eyes, Nanuk left his igloo home. Just as she had said, the old woman's heart felt like it had broken.

The old woman missed her son. She soon became thin and pale with sorrow.

The children also missed their lost friend, and the village became an unhappy place. The men began to feel deeply ashamed of their actions.

One day, when the old woman's heart ached with sadness, she decided to set out to find Nanuk. She left at dawn and walked all day across the icy plains. As she walked, she called out Nanuk's name. After hours of searching, she saw her polar bear son running toward her. He had grown big and strong in the time he had been gone, and his white fur shimmered in the northern light.

"Nanuk!" the old woman cried, and she wrapped her arms around him.

Nanuk could see how tired and hungry his mother looked, so he caught some fish for her to eat and carved a snow den with his paws to keep her warm. They stayed together for a day and a night, then Nanuk carried his mother home.

When the villagers saw Nanuk and realized how far the old woman must have traveled to be with him, they bowed their heads with shame. From then on, Nanuk visited his mother every day, and the whole village welcomed him. They had learned that the love between a mother and her child should always be treated with respect. ⊚

Maui Goes Fishing

Maui's four older brothers never let him join in their fun. One morning, they all rose with the sun to go deep-sea fishing in their special canoe.

"Please let me come with you," begged Maui, but his older brothers just laughed at him and teased him. "One day, little boy, but not today. There isn't enough room in our canoe for you as well as all the fish we're planning to bring home with us!"

Maui had a secret. He had magic powers that his family didn't know about. While his brothers got their fishing gear ready, he came up with a plan to use his magic. When he was a baby, he had been given an enchanted jawbone by the ocean spirits. He hid it in a secret box.

He took out the jawbone from his secret box and used it to make a fishing hook. Then, he braided some flax into a fishing line, and he climbed into a basket at the bottom of their canoe.

When at last the four brothers were ready to set out, they grumbled about how much heavier the canoe felt.

While they were far out at sea fishing, one of the brothers grabbed the basket to put a fish in—and uncovered Maui. "Little squirt!" he said. "You tricked us! We're taking you back to shore right now!"

The brothers took up their paddles again, but Maui wished on his magic fishhook that the seashore would look further and further away. After 10 minutes of paddling, the brothers were so tired, they gave up.

"Keep out of our way, pipsqueak," they grumbled, and the brothers cast their fishing lines into the sea.

Maui stayed down at the bottom end of the canoe, hoping that his brothers wouldn't see what he was up to. He quietly dropped the magic fishhook over the edge of the boat.

Suddenly, Maui felt a powerful tug on his line. The tug was so strong that Maui feared he might be dragged into the water!

"Brothers! Quick, help me!" he cried, gripping his fishing line tightly. The four brothers dashed toward Maui just as the canoe was about to capsize, and together, they heaved and tugged on the line with all their might. To their great surprise, a hunk of land surfaced before them. It was shaped like a fish. Maui had caught New Zealand's North Island! Maui was worried that the ocean spirits would be angry with him for catching the island. He dived into the sea to ask for their forgiveness. Before he went, he asked his brothers to guard the island.

While Maui was under water, his greedy brothers started to hack and chop at the fish-shaped land, trying to claim little bits of it for themselves. This is why New Zealand's North Island is so craggy and mountainous.

After performing the miracle of catching North Island, Maui became famous among the Maori people. He grew up to be a much-loved personality. And to this day, the North Island of New Zealand is also known as Te Ika A Maui—or Maui's Fish. ᓂ

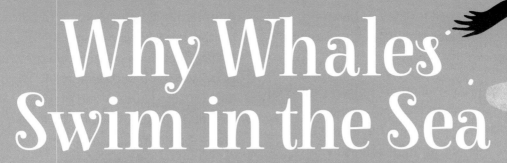

Why Whales Swim in the Sea

Long ago in far-off Patagonia, the whale was a giant of an animal who lived on land. She had four little legs and was known as Goos.

Goos lived in the grassy meadows, near to a group of people known as the Tehuelche. Goos liked the Tehuelche folk, and they liked her, too. Because Goos was so big and heavy and her legs were so small, she couldn't move around much. She spent most of her time sitting in the grass, watching the world go by. She liked to watch the cougars stalking past and look at the condors flying in the sky. Sometimes, she'd watch the people going about their business.

One day, Goos watched the young members of the Tehuelche heading off for a day of hunting, and she began to feel restless. "Oh, I wish it wasn't so difficult to walk around," she sighed. "I wish I could see more of the world—just like these people do."

Poor, bored Goos broke into a huge yawn. Her mouth was so big and her breath so strong, she accidentally sucked in the trees, all the huts in front of her, and all of the remaining Tehuelche villagers! When she opened her eyes, she wondered why everyone was gone!

With nothing to look at anymore, Goos lumbered away to the woods, where she fell fast asleep. When the hunters returned later that day, they were shocked to find that their homes and families were gone. "Thieves!" they cried. "Kidnappers!" they all shouted. "Where are our families?"

But the bravest and wisest of the Tehuelche people, a man named Elal, calmed everyone down and offered to lead the search for their missing villagers. He spotted a huge patch in the meadow where the grass had been flattened and saw a trail of footprints. *Goos!* he thought.

Elal followed the trail into the woods and saw the snoozing whale. As he drew nearer, the leaves crunched beneath his feet, and Goos moved and let out a giant yawn. Elal was shocked to see that as Goos yawned, she sucked in the branches of the tree in front of her, along with some birds that were nesting there.

Elal ran toward the whale and shook her as hard as he could. "Goos!" he cried. "Goos, you must wake up!"

But Goos was fast asleep and having a lovely dream about floating in the air, as light as a feather. Goos let out another yawn, and this time, Elal leapt into the whale's mouth and tiptoed nervously into her stomach.

In the darkness, he could just make out the Tehuelche villagers huddled in a corner. Their belongings were scattered all around, and there was even a horse in there! His people were completely overjoyed to see him.

"OK, everyone, grab what you can, then we must tickle Goos to make her stir. When I say so, everyone run toward Goos's mouth and jump out!"

Elal took the horse by its reins, and they all tickled inside Goos's tummy. Sleepy Goos twitched and yawned again, and her prisoners sprinted out and leaped onto the ground.

When Goos woke up later, Elal was waiting to speak to her. He told her what had happened, and Goos felt terribly sorry. But Elal had an idea.

"You know, we're not far from the sea, Goos. You could live there. The water will support the weight of your body, and you'll be able to see the world!"

Goos thought this was a brilliant plan. The next morning, Goos, Elal, and the Tehuelche people set off for the beach. When Goos walked into the sea, the feeling of water supporting her body was so wonderful, she realized that she was truly home. She said farewell to her friends and began the exciting life of adventure she had always longed for. And that is why whales swim in the sea!

Smell of Soup, Sound of Money

Once, in the city of Ankara in Turkey, there was a poor old beggar who had nothing in the world but the clothes on his back.

One day, he was begging on the street when a shopkeeper threw out a stale slice of bread. The beggar grabbed it before the birds could peck at it. As he walked the streets, chewing at the tough, dry crust of bread, he thought, *How nice it would be to have something to eat with this bread.* And he started to dream of bean stew and lentil soup.

Just then, he walked past an inn. *Perhaps this innkeeper will take pity on me*, he thought.

"Please madam, can you spare something that I can eat with this bread?"

"Do you have any money to pay for my food?" asked the innkeeper.

"Not a single coin, I'm afraid," said the poor beggar.

"Then, get out of here before I throw you out!" shouted the innkeeper, and she waved her fist at him.

Fearing that the innkeeper would chase after him, the disappointed beggar ducked down the alleyway on the side of the inn. There, he found the entrance to the inn's kitchen. He smelled something delicious.

The beggar carefully stepped inside, where he found a large pot of bean soup bubbling away over the fire.

I'm not a thief, thought the beggar, *but this soup smells so delicious it makes me ache all over with hunger. Perhaps I could hold my bread over it, and some of the nice smell will soak in and give it a bit of flavor.*

And so, the beggar held his bread over the steaming hot soup.

At that very moment, the innkeeper stormed into the kitchen, crying out, "Stop! You are stealing my special soup!"

"But I have stolen nothing!" cried the beggar. "I was just enjoying its smell and hoping that its lovely aroma might make my dry bread taste a bit better."

"Then, you must pay me for the smell!" said the innkeeper. But of course, she knew that the beggar was penniless.

"Can't pay up, eh?" she grinned. "Right, it's off to the judge with you!" And she seized the beggar by the arm and dragged him to the local courthouse.

Now, at that time, Nasreddin Hodja was the judge, and he was known for being fair and wise. Hodja listened patiently to the innkeeper's account of what had happened.

When she had finished, Hodja said, "So, let me get this straight. You are asking

this man, who I am guessing has no home, no possessions, and no money, to pay for the smell of soup from your kitchen?"

"Indeed," said the innkeeper. "I think it's only fair."

The judge nodded. "Very well then, I will pay what this poor beggar owes you, but only if you agree to drop your charges against him," he said.

The innkeeper nodded and smiled smugly at the thought of getting some

money. Meanwhile, the beggar fell to his knees and thanked the judge for his great kindness.

Hodja then took out several coins, jingled them in his hands, then put them back in his pocket.

The innkeeper looked confused.

"There," said Hodja, smiling. "I have paid for the smell of your soup with the sound of money." Then, he sent the disappointed innkeeper on her way and invited the beggar to lunch. ⟨⟩

The Mouse Merchant

In a small Indian town, there lived a boy and his poor widowed mother. Though they hadn't a penny to their name, the boy's mother had done her best to give her son a good education.

On the boy's thirteenth birthday, his mother said, "When your father was alive, he was a merchant. It is time for you to follow in his steps. There is a rich merchant called Visakhila who lives in the next town. He lends money to people who want to make better lives for themselves. Please go to him and ask for a loan to get you started."

The boy was excited at the thought of being a merchant like his father, so he set off without delay.

When he arrived at Visakhila's house, he heard an angry voice shout, "I gave you many rupees, and you have simply wasted them all! Do you see that dead mouse on the floor? Someone could take even that and turn it into money!"

At that, the boy stepped into the room and said, "I accept your challenge! I will take that mouse as my loan from you!" He put it in his pocket and wrote out a receipt for the merchant.

The merchant and the young man he had been scolding both looked on in shock and then burst into laughter.

However, when the boy left, the merchant put the receipt in his safe.

As he walked down the road, the boy met a trader who had an unhappy cat. "I'll give this dead mouse to your cat to play with, in exchange for some goods from your stall," said the boy. The trader was so grateful, he gave the boy two large handfuls of chickpea flour and a pitcher.

The boy used the chickpea flour to make delicious flatbreads. He filled the pitcher with spring water. Then, he set himself up in a shady spot on the road between the forest and the town gates.

At the end of the day, many hungry and thirsty woodcutters came out of the forest. The boy gave them some flatbreads and water. In return, each woodcutter gave him some wood.

The next day, the boy sold some of his wood at the market to buy more flour to make more flatbreads. He stored the rest of the rupees in his purse.

He did this for many weeks until he had built up a huge supply of wood, and his purse was filled with money.

When a cold spell arrived and people were shivering in their homes, the boy was able to sell all of the wood he had stored away for a very good price.

He had enough money to set himself up as a merchant with his own shop. He even had a room for his mother to live in. With hard work, honesty, and intelligence, the boy soon grew into a wealthy young man, and customers came from far and wide to buy his goods.

One day, when he knew that he had truly made his fortune, he visited the local jeweler and asked him to make a mouse of solid gold. The young man delivered the golden mouse to Visakhila to repay his debt.

At first, Visakhila was confused, but then he remembered the old receipt at the back of his safe and the boy who had once picked up a dead mouse from his floor. Visakhila laughed and congratulated the young man on his success. From that day on, he became famous throughout India as the Mouse Merchant! ᕫ

The Shark God

Long ago, the ocean around Fiji was bothered by an angry shark god who went by the name of Dakuwaqa.

At that time, the ocean was full of guardian gods. Some guarded the fish, some guarded the eels, and some guarded the turtles. Dakuwaqa guarded the coral reefs. He was a greedy god—greedy for power—and he loved to show off his strength.

"There is no ocean god stronger than I am!" he boasted. He took pleasure in challenging any god who crossed his path to a fight. His first battle was with the barracuda god, who was famous for his sharp teeth. When the two gods fought, the waves they created were so huge that they crashed over the beaches of Fiji and flooded many villages.

The shark god won this battle and many more. Soon, the other gods feared him so much they swam away when they saw him coming. Humans were so scared of him, they no longer swam in the ocean, and fishermen stopped going to sea.

"Ha!" bragged Dakuwaqa. "Everyone fears me. I am all-powerful!"

.△.△.△.△.

One day, Dakuwaqa was visited by a lesser shark god called Masilaca.

"Good day, Dakuwaqa. I do not wish to fight—I know you are the strongest. I thought I would tell you of a god you might like to challenge."

"I have already challenged everyone who is worth fighting," said Dakuwaqa, full of arrogance. "But who is this god?"

"It is a deadly giant with many arms, and it guards a small island to the east of Fiji. They say it is the most powerful god in the ocean."

"Nonsense!" sneered Dakuwaqa. "I am the strongest and I will prove it."

Masilaca was hoping Dakuwaqa would have this reaction.

Dakuwaqa was eager to meet this new challenger. He swam to the island mentioned by the shark Masilaca. On the beach, an old man was fishing.

"Old man!" called the shark god. "Where is the puny god that guards your island?"

"He lives on the south side, where he guards a difficult passage between the rocks. He is bold and brave. He looks after our people, and you will find him hard to beat." The old man was not afraid of Dakuwaqa, and this angered the shark god.

"Nonsense!" he snapped. "There is no ocean god stronger than I am!"

He sped through the water toward the rocky passage. When he drew near, he shouted a warning, "Make way, guardian, I am coming through!"

A deep, booming voice answered. "Not without my permission."

Dakuwaqa charged ahead, but slammed into the body of a giant octopus.

"I am Rokobakaniceva," said the octopus. "I am the god of this island reef. You will not pass and cause trouble for the creatures here."

Dakuwaqa rushed at Rokobakaniceva again, baring his deadly teeth. But the octopus god blocked the passage

with his huge body and used four of his tentacles to grip the rocks around him. He coiled his remaining tentacles around the shark god and squeezed as tightly as he could.

Dakuwaqa wriggled and writhed. He gnashed and snapped his teeth, but the octopus had him in a strong hold. He could not escape. He thought his lungs might cave in from the pressure.

"Please, let me go!" he gasped. "I promise I will leave and never return."

"You must promise more than that," said the octopus god.

"I promise you I will never harm the creatures or humans who live here," said Dakuwaqa.

"Good," said the octopus god. "You must keep this promise, or I will hunt you and punish you." At last, he released his grip on Dakuwaqa.

The shark god was so scared and so ashamed he had been beaten, he swam away at great speed, leaving the octopus god chuckling to himself.

To this day, Dakuwaqa keeps his word, and the people of Fiji can fish and swim without coming to any harm.

27

How the Milky Way Came to Be

Long ago, when the land of Estonia was new, Uko, the great god of nature, put his daughter Lindu in charge of all the birds.

Lindu knew everything there was to know about her feathered friends, including all the paths they should follow in spring and autumn and the best places to make their nests. She cared for the birds as though they were her children, and she was always there to guide them.

Lindu was also a great beauty and had attracted the attention of suitors from far and wide. One night, the North Star drove up in his bronze carriage drawn by six chestnut horses. He gave Lindu 10 gifts and asked her if she would marry him.

"I can't marry you," replied Lindu. "I need to be free as a bird, and you must always stay in one place."

The North Star drove away sadly.

The following night, the Moon drove up in a silver carriage drawn by six dapple-gray horses. He had with him 20 gifts, and he asked for Lindu's hand in marriage.

"I can't marry you," replied Lindu. "I need to be free as a bird, and you always follow the same path."

The Moon drove away in sorrow.

The next morning, the Sun drove up in a golden carriage drawn by six golden horses. He offered Lindu thirty gifts and asked her to be his bride.

"I can't marry you," replied Lindu. "I need to be free as a bird, and you are like the moon. You follow the same path every day."

The Sun drove away, weeping golden tears.

That night, the Northern Lights drove up in a jewelled carriage drawn by 100 white horses. Lindu was truly dazzled. He gave her 100 gifts, but these were of no interest because she had already fallen in love.

When the Northern Lights asked Lindu to marry him, she replied, "You move across the skies freely, and you wear robes as beautiful as the birds. I will be happy to be your bride."

Daylight was coming, and he had to get home, so the Northern Lights said farewell to Lindu and promised to return soon for their wedding and to carry her north to live with him.

The next day, Lindu began to prepare for the wedding. The birds gave her their softest and most delicate feathers for her bridal gown. She looked beautiful.

She sat and waited eagerly for her groom, but he didn't appear—and he didn't come the next night, or the one

after that. One day followed another, and the Northern Lights didn't return because he was ever changing and couldn't keep his promise.

Winter passed and spring came. Lindu became so sad that she forgot her duty to the birds, who flapped about, unsure of where to migrate to or where to nest.

The birds began to sing in distress. Their song carried on the breeze to the nature god, Uko, who told the four winds to carry Lindu to his palace in the heavens.

When Uko saw how heartbroken his daughter was, he realized that living on Earth would always make her sad. He gave her a home in the heavens and made her the Milky Way.

Her long white wedding veil and gown sweep and stretch across the sky. From her seat, she can tell the birds where they must go on their migrations. She can sometimes see the Northern Lights, and she waves to him from afar. If you watch carefully, you might see the Northern Lights wave back at her, too.

Book Club Questions

1. In which tales do the settings affect the actions and outcomes of the characters? Which tales could take place anywhere and still have the same outcomes?

2. What role does jealousy play in "The Polar Bear Son"? How does a mother's love overcome jealousy and redeem the village?

3. Compare "Maui Goes Fishing" and "How The Milky Way Came to Be." How are the tales alike and different?

4. Contrast the heroes in "Why Whales Swim in the Sea" and "The Shark God." How do they solve the problems facing them?

5. In "Smell of Soup, Sound of Money," how is the innkeeper's ingenious plan foiled?

6. What do the main characters in "Smell of Soup, Sound of Money" and "The Mouse Merchant" have in common?